Each One Precious

by
Natasha Stonehouse

Image interior credit : Natasha Stonehouse

WestBow Press books may be ordered through booksellers or by contacting:

WestBow Press
A Division of Thomas Nelson & Zondervan
1663 Liberty Drive
Bloomington, IN 47403
www.westbowpress.com
1 (866) 928-1240

ISBN: 978-1-5127-9296-6 (sc)
ISBN: 978-1-5127-9297-3 (e)

Library of Congress Control Number: 2017909983

Print information available on the last page.

WestBow Press rev. date: 06/27/2017

WESTBOW
PRESS®
A DIVISION OF THOMAS NELSON
& ZONDERVAN

Each One Precious

To the children of the Gracia ministry in San Isidro, Santa Cruz Bolivia: May you always know how precious you are to God, that he has a purpose for your life and that he has created you different and special for a reason. May you shine his light in the world.

To Yandira and Ed: As you share God's love with children of the Gracia ministry may God fill you every day with his overwhelming love. You are exactly where you are meant to be. It is a blessing to partner with you in this tiny way.

To the Vargas family: Some families are knit together by blood, others are created in the heart. I will forever be thankful that God allowed me the privilege to be a part of yours.

A portion of the author's proceeds from the sale of every book will be donated to the Gracia ministry in San Isidro, Santa Cruz, Bolivia. For more information of the ministry please see their Facebook page at https://www.facebook.com/ministeriograciabolivia

Special thanks to:

-My friends and family for encouraging and
sometimes pushing me to pursue this project.
-Mellary Bitner for doing the layout and
type setting throughout the book. I
could not have done it without you.
-Aletta Luma and Heather Pitman
for helping with editing.
-My Heavenly Father for giving me the idea
in the first place. Thank you for reminding
me that I am incredibly loved and can serve
you regardless of my lumps and bumps.

Way up north where the air is cold, where the wind blows over the hills and through the trees, lived a village of gentle snowmen.

Each of the snowmen was different, but all were made by the same creator. Andrew had large branches for arms instead of little sticks.

Everyone in the village knew that if there was something heavy that needed lifting they could call Andrew. His arms were strong, and he was always willing to help.

When there was a problem
in the village the snowmen
would go to Mary.

She could look at mysteries that others could not solve and was able to figure them out.

Her mind was sharp, and her heart was kind.

The littlest of the snowmen
brought joy to each villager.

Timothy's playful antics
and contagious laughter
echoed off the hills
bringing smiles to the
faces of all who heard it.

No one was sad in
his presence.

And then there was Isabel.

She didn't have thick, strong branches and couldn't lift heavy things like Andrew.

She couldn't solve problems quickly like Mary.

She didn't make everyone laugh like Timothy.

What she did have was lumpy snow.

The others often commented on her bumps and lumps and after a while Isabel thought that there was nothing that she was good at.

One evening Isabel climbed the hill overlooking the village to talk to her creator, "God, I am not strong like Andrew, as smart as Mary or as funny as Timothy.

Why did you have to make me this way?
All I have is bumps."

God's voice was deep and kind.

"Isabel, look at the snowmen in the village.
Each one different.
Each one precious.
Each one loved by me and each one with a purpose.

They can shine my light in the world.
YOU can shine my light."

It was then that Isabel noticed the
moonlight shining off her bumpy snow.

The snow glimmered like diamonds.

"God," she exclaimed, "My snow.
It's beautiful. I'm beautiful!"

"Of course. You are mine. I made you, and I don't make mistakes. What others see as a mistake I use to shine my light."

Isabel sat in the moonlight, with
her snow glittering like diamonds,
feeling overwhelmingly loved.

She was determined to listen only to the voice
of her creator and shine His light in the world-
lumps,

bumps

and all.

CPSIA information can be obtained
at www.ICGtesting.com
Printed in the USA
LVOW05s1749140717
540884LV00012BA/20/P